W9-BMF-767
BLUE MOSQUE
ISTANBUL - TURKEY
WELCOME TO
NEW YORK CITY
WELCOME TO
FCB
ישראל
PETERSBURG
HAWAII
Aloha
HAWAII
BRANDENBURG
GERMANY
DESTINATIONS
DUBLIN
VENICE
VENICE
ROMA
BRAZIL
VANCOUVER CANADA
Vancouver
CHINA BEIJING CHINA
Beijing
EDINBURGH
UK
EDINBURGH
Scotland

Cairo
SAINT PETERSBURG
RUSSIA
FAMOUS
DESTINATIONS
CANADA
Vancouver
ROMA
ITALY
FCB
BERLIN
GERMANY
EDINBURGH
UK
EDINBURGH
Scotland
VENICE
VENICE
ישראל
WELCOME
NEW YORK CITY
WELCOME TO
CHINA
Beijing
HAWAII
Aloha
HAWAII
BLUE MOSQUE
ISTANBUL - TURKEY

THIS BOOK BELONGS TO

Christmas in New York City!

Written by
Lisa Manzione

Illustrated by
Kristine Lucco

Bella & Harry, LLC

JULY
IV
MDCCLXXVI

"**Faster,** Santa... faster! Wwwwwwwwhhhhhhhheeeeeee!" Bella cried with excitement, as she and Harry rode with Santa Claus in his sleigh across the New York City (NYC) skyline.

Suddenly, Bella opened her eyes and realized she was only dreaming. For a moment, she felt sad, but then Bella realized she really was in New York City with Harry and their family!

Bella darted out of her dog bed, looked out the hotel window, and saw the beautiful snow-covered city street below. Quickly, Bella ran to the other window, which looked out to the most famous street in Manhattan... Fifth Avenue!

"Oh, Harry, I just love Manhattan at Christmastime! All of the beautiful lights, decorations, and storefront windows. It is just magical here this time of year!"

"Manhattan, Bella? I thought we were in New York City."

5 Boroughs 1 City

"We are, Harry. New York City is made up of five boroughs... Manhattan, Brooklyn, Queens, Staten Island, and the Bronx. We will be spending our time in Manhattan while we are visiting here."

"Let's take a look at our map before we start our walk. The state of New York is located in the northeastern part of the United States but is considered a mid-Atlantic state. Here, you can see exactly where both the state of New York and the city of New York are located."

"**Harry,** put on your scarf. We are leaving for our walk down Fifth Avenue! This avenue has many national historic landmarks such as St. Patrick's Cathedral, the Empire State Building, and the famous New York Public Library, which has lions guarding the front doors!"

"**Today,** we are going to walk from East 59th Street, down Fifth Avenue, to Rockefeller Center, passing all of the fancy store windows along the way."

"**Look!** I see a real walking toy soldier! Look over there! I see a building that looks like a box made out of Christmas lights!"

"**We** have arrived at Rockefeller Center. Look at the beautiful horn-blowing angels. The angels line The Channel Gardens and make a perfect frame for the tree."

"WOW!

Look at the tree, Harry! How pretty!"

"**The** first official tree was put up in 1933. A tree has been put up here every year since then. There are thousands and thousands of lights on the tree. Everyone who comes to Manhattan at Christmastime must see the famous Rockefeller Center Christmas Tree!"

"**Look!** I see Prometheus! Do you see him? He is watching over the ice skating rink! Let's go! How fun! We can ice skate under the Christmas tree while Prometheus watches over us!"

"Who, Bella?"

"**Prometheus.** He was a god in mythology and it is said he brought fire to mankind. Greek mythology can be a lot of fun to study, but right now... it's all about Christmas in New York City! Harry, put your skates on! Our family is already out on the ice!"

"**Whew!** I am tired.
That was so much fun!"

"Snack time!"

"Our family is stopping at a street vendor to buy a snack. Look at all of the choices! I see hot dogs and pretzels and nuts. Look over there! Chestnuts are roasting! Oh, Harry, this is a great place to visit!"

"Let's go, Harry. We are walking to Radio City Music Hall. We are going to see the legendary Rockettes, and watch the show, too!"

"Bella, I didn't know rockets were kept at radio stations."

"Oh, Harry, we are not talking about rockets or radio stations! Radio City Music Hall is an indoor theater that was opened to the public in 1932. The Music Hall is open for concerts, stage shows, and dance shows. The Rockettes are ladies that perform and dance, not only at Radio City Music Hall, but other places, too."

"Picture time!"

"Ohhhh....

Wooden Soldiers, Harry! Da... da... da... march, march, march... da... da... da! There is the cannon! Bang!"

"Bella, that was so cool... they all fell down in a row!"

"Times Square is the next stop on our tour."

"**Does** someone tell you the time in the square, Bella?"

"Well, yes, there is a big clock in the square, but Times Square is really an area in Manhattan which is the center of the Broadway Theater District. That means there are lots of places where you can see live plays on stage."

"Let's go, Harry. We are going to walk from Times Square to West 34th Street."

"One of the largest department stores in the United States is located here. I think they have the best window decorations in the entire world at Christmastime!"

"**WOW!** Harry, look at this window! No, quick... look at this window! No, this window! Oh, Harry, I don't know where to look first. I just love it here, Harry, don't you? Let's head inside so we can have our picture taken with Santa Claus."

"**Hi** Santa Claus, I'm Harry. I really want a big, juicy bone for Christmas!"

"Ho Ho Ho, you're a very cute puppy, Harry!"

"**Harry,** did you bring the letters we wrote to Santa Claus?"

"Yes, I did, Bella!"

"Great! Let's drop the letters in the North Pole Mailbox. We want to make sure Santa Claus remembers what is on our list!"

Christmas in New York City is the most magical place in the world! We had a great time and hope you did also! Merry Christmas to all from Bella Boo and Harry too!

NYC

Our Christmas Adventures in New York City

Bella and Harry enjoying a ride in a New York City taxicab.

Bella and Harry sipping "frozen hot chocolate."

Bella and Harry in Central Park with their friend, Molly (a Cavalier King Charles Spaniel). Molly enjoys traveling as much as Bella and Harry do!

Bella and Harry in Grand Central Terminal Station (a big train station in Manhattan).

Bella, very tired, after a full day of shopping in the Big Apple (another name for New York City)!

Merry Christmas!

Library of Congress Cataloging-in-Publications Data is available

Manzione, Lisa

The Adventures of Bella & Harry: Christmas in New York City!

ISBN: 978-1-937616-58-8

First Edition

Book Eighteen of Bella & Harry Series

For further information please visit:

BellaAndHarry.com

or

Email: BellaAndHarryGo@aol.com

Printed in the United States of America

Phoenix Color, Hagerstown, Maryland

April 2015

15 4 18 PC 1 1

BLUE MOSQUE
ISTANBUL - TURKEY
WELCOME TO
NEW YORK CITY
WELCOME TO
Cairo
FCB
ישראל
PETERSBURG
HAWAII
Aloha
HAWAII
BRANDENBURG
GERMANY
DESTINATIONS
DUBLIN
VENICE
VENICE
ROMA
BRAZIL
VANCOUVER CANADA
Vancouver
CHINA BEIJING CHINA
Beijing
EDINBURGH
UK
EDINBURGH
Scotland

SAINT PETERSBURG
RUSSIA
FAMOUS
DESTINATIONS
Cairo
CANADA
Vancouver
ROMA
ITALY
FCB
BERLIN
GATE
EDINBURGH
UK
Scotland
VENICE
WELCOME TO
HAWAII
Aloha
HAWAII
CHINA
Beijing
BLUE MOSQUE
ISTANBUL - TURKEY
ישראל